Dear Parents and Educators,

Welcome to Penguin Young Readers! As parents and educators, you know that each child develops at his or her own pace—in terms of speech, critical thinking, and, of course, reading. Penguin Young Readers recognizes this fact. As a result, each Penguin Young Readers book is assigned a traditional easy-to-read level (1–4) as well as a Guided Reading Level (A–P). Both of these systems will help you choose the right book for your child. Please refer to the back of each book for specific leveling information. Penguin Young Readers features esteemed authors and illustrators, stories about favorite characters, fascinating nonfiction, and more!

Tiny the Snow Dog

LEVEL **1**

GUIDED
READING **D**
LEVEL

This book is perfect for an **Emergent Reader** who:
- can read in a left-to-right and top-to-bottom progression;
- can recognize some beginning and ending letter sounds;
- can use picture clues to help tell the story; and
- can understand the basic plot and sequence of simple stories.

Here are some **activities** you can do during and after reading this book:
- Character Traits: Tiny is a dog, but he certainly is *not* tiny. Write down a list of words that describe Tiny.
- Make Connections: What would you do if you were outside playing with Tiny and could not find him? Where would you look for him?
- Make Predictions: What do you think Tiny and the boy will do after they warm up inside? Will they go outside to play in the snow again? If so, what activities will they do? Or, if they stay inside, what will they do for fun?

Remember, sharing the love of reading with a child is the best gift you can give!

—Bonnie Bader, EdM
Penguin Young Readers program

*Penguin Young Readers are leveled by independent reviewers applying the standards developed by Irene Fountas and Gay Su Pinnell in *Matching Books to Readers: Using Leveled Books in Guided Reading*, Heinemann, 1999.

For John—CM

To the One who loves all the children of
the world—Jesus Christ, my Redeemer—RD

Penguin Young Readers
Published by the Penguin Group
Penguin Group (USA) Inc., 375 Hudson Street, New York, New York 10014, USA
Penguin Group (Canada), 90 Eglinton Avenue East, Suite 700, Toronto, Ontario M4P 2Y3, Canada
(a division of Pearson Penguin Canada Inc.)
Penguin Books Ltd., 80 Strand, London WC2R 0RL, England
Penguin Group Ireland, 25 St. Stephen's Green, Dublin 2, Ireland (a division of Penguin Books Ltd.)
Penguin Group (Australia), 250 Camberwell Road, Camberwell, Victoria 3124, Australia
(a division of Pearson Australia Group Pty. Ltd.)
Penguin Books India Pvt. Ltd., 11 Community Centre, Panchsheel Park, New Delhi—110 017, India
Penguin Group (NZ), 67 Apollo Drive, Rosedale, Auckland 0632, New Zealand
(a division of Pearson New Zealand Ltd.)
Penguin Books (South Africa) (Pty.) Ltd., 24 Sturdee Avenue,
Rosebank, Johannesburg 2196, South Africa

Penguin Books Ltd., Registered Offices: 80 Strand, London WC2R 0RL, England

Text copyright © 2001 by Cari Meister. Illustrations copyright © 2001 by Rich Davis.
All rights reserved. First published in 2001 by Viking and Puffin Books, imprints of Penguin Group
(USA) Inc. Published in 2011 by Penguin Young Readers, an imprint of Penguin Group (USA) Inc.,
345 Hudson Street, New York, New York 10014. Manufactured in China.

The Library of Congress has cataloged the Viking edition
under the following Control Number: 99088385

ISBN 978-0-14-056708-3   10 9 8 7 6 5 4 3 2 1

PENGUIN YOUNG READERS

LEVEL

1

EMERGENT READER

Tiny the Snow Dog

by Cari Meister
illustrated by Rich Davis

Penguin Young Readers
An Imprint of Penguin Group (USA) Inc.

This is Tiny.

He is my dog.

Tiny loves winter.

I do, too.

Look, Tiny! Snow!

Tiny wants to go out.

I do, too.

Brrr! It is cold.

We need warm hats.

Tiny has a new hat.

I do, too.

Ready? Go!

I toss a snowball.

Tiny runs.

Tiny runs and runs.

Oh no! Where is Tiny?

I do not see him.

I look by the barn.

No Tiny.

I look by the hill.

No Tiny.

I look and look and look.

Still no Tiny.

Tiny, where are you?

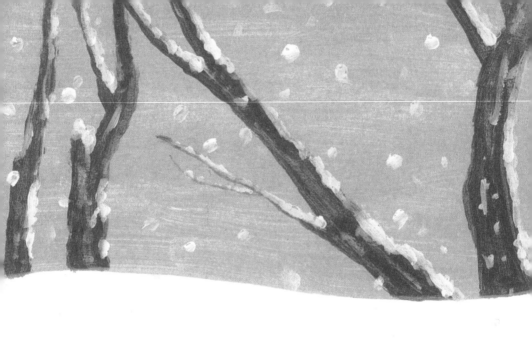

Crunch, crunch, crunch.

What is that?

Crunch, crunch, crunch.

A snow monster.

A snow monster is

coming to get me!

Slurp!

It is Tiny!

Tiny is the snow monster.

Come on, Tiny.

Time to go home.

Good snow dog.